SCREAM AT THE FAIR

THE TWISTED SOCIETY

CRISTINA LOLLABRIGIDA

This is a work of fiction. Names, characters, places, and incidents either are the product of the author's imagination or are used fictitiously. Any resemblance to actual persons, living or dead, events, or locales is entirely coincidental.

Edited & Proofread by Sarah EA Hart - Little Darlings

Cover design by Getcovers

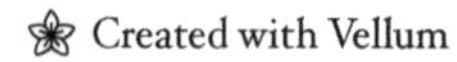
Created with Vellum

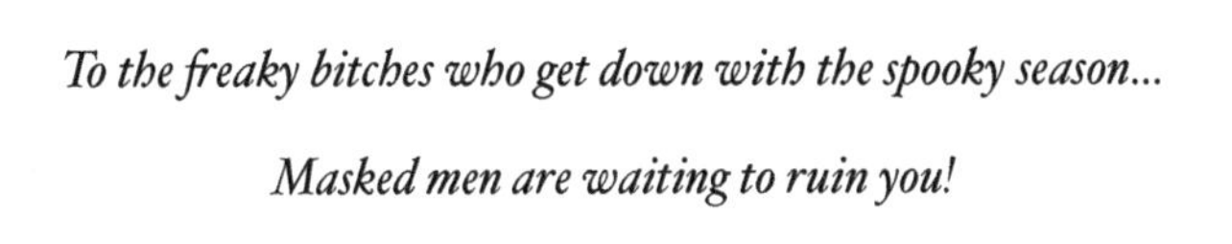

To the freaky bitches who get down with the spooky season...

Masked men are waiting to ruin you!

BLURB

Tallulah Daniels has been contacted by the mysterious Society. A $100,000 prize is hers if she can survive 12 hours in the abandoned fairgrounds. It should be easy for a horror movie buff to spend her Halloween being scared by actors.

It turns out to be more than jump scares and costume makeup. She's trapped in a sensual nightmare and pushed to her limits. When quitting isn't an option, will the seductive Lucien turn out to be friend or foe as Tallulah attempts to elude her masked hunters?

"Scream at the Fair" is a holiday-based erotic novella. Intended for readers 18+. Includes triggers.

CONTENT/TRIGGER WARNING

Scream at the Fair is an erotic, horror novella intended for readers 18+.

Triggers may include:

Strong language, violence, blood/gore, stalking/hunting, non-consensual sex, non-consensual drugging, explicit sexual content including bondage, knife play, blood play, spitting, primal play, breath play, and more. Terrors brought to life include being buried alive and waterboarding.

YOU HAVE BEEN CHOSEN

A KNOCK SOUNDED from Tallulah Daniels's townhouse door. A courier dressed in black with a phantom mask handed her a black envelope adorned with silver filigree and no return address.

He prompted her to sign and offer a fingerprint scan to confirm her identity. With a dumbfounded goodbye, Tallulah closed her door. She swept aside the curtain from the small window near the door and watched the man climb into a black town car and drive away into the night before her attention fell back to the envelope burning in her hands.

Tallulah's hands shook as she opened the envelope. She sliced the pad of her finger on the flap and winced slightly.

"Damn, paper cut," she said before sucking the bead of blood into her mouth. The tangy, metallic taste ignited a certain hunger within her. But that would have to wait as she removed the heavy cardstock with perfectly scripted calligraphy.

Congratulations, Tallulah Daniels,

You have been hand-selected by The Society to participate in this October's thrill challenge. If you choose to accept this invitation, you will be eligible to win a $100,000 prize. Can you survive 12 hours locked inside an abandoned fairground?

Scan the code below—if you dare.

Everyone knew about The Society, as it was referred to—the *elite* who ruled the country as puppet masters. But the public had no knowledge of who made up this secret organization. The Society was spoken of in reverent tones, and naysayers disappeared off the streets, never to be seen again.

They hosted pop-up events multiple times a year in different parts of the country. The names of every person between the ages of 18 and 35 were entered into a lottery. Every night for a week, names were drawn. Those chosen received an exclusive invitation to participate in the challenge.

The money would be life-changing for her. Tallulah imagined the financial independence she could achieve with the prize money. Her ex had run up her credit cards and left her with thousands to pay on top of her student loans and her late mother's medical bills.

Her eagerness was about to be challenged as she scanned the code with her phone. A black screen popped up, and she tapped the play button. A horror-themed music box melody began to play while graphic images flashed so quickly that her eyes couldn't focus.

A blood-curdling scream cut through the music, causing Tallulah to jump. The black screen gave way to a petite blonde-haired woman who was strapped spread-eagle on a metal table. She screamed again as a vampiress bit into her neck. The vampiress licked the blood that dripped from the wounds her teeth had created.

A creepy clown appeared behind her and said something that wasn't picked up over the woman's sobs. He slid a gag into her mouth. A demon wearing a large strap-on stepped between her legs and positioned himself at both of her holes. Her hands clenched, and her body went rigid as the creature thrust forward. Her screams were muffled by the red rubber ball between her teeth as the demon showed no mercy in his movements.

The screen went black again. A timestamp showing two hours and thirty-seven minutes flashed before disappearing. The words—*Do you have what it takes, Tallulah Daniels?*—floated across the screen. She clicked the button and filled out the form.

Once she finished, she took her vibrator from the bottom drawer of her nightstand and conjured a scene in her mind. She replaced the woman in the video with herself. Her breath quickened as she cantered her hips against the high setting of the buzzy toy.

The vampiress sucked and licked at her skin while the double-cocked demon worked as hard as her vibrator. They called her a dirty little slut, which only spurred her on.

"Yes," she cried.

Come for us, they demanded. And she was all too happy to oblige. Tallulah's core clamped down on the toy, and she moved her other hand to her clit. Aftershocks pulsed through her as the demon pulled out and came on her stomach. She wore that like a badge of honor.

CHAPTER 1

ONE MONTH LATER...

TALLULAH SAT in a nondescript room across from a middle-aged lawyer who sniffed at the end of every sentence. Her eyes threatened to roll back from boredom as he droned on for over an hour, reading through the contract. By signing, she agreed to spend 12 hours locked within the haunted fair-grounds to compete for the $100,000 prize.

"What does this mean that the actors are allowed to fulfill their most basic and primitive urges?"

"Primitive urges include hunger, thirst, anger, *and* sex. When these needs are not met, the result is usually a state of anxiety or tension."

"Am I in danger?"

Tallulah was the last chosen contestant for the Fair event and the only female. How would she last for 12 hours if six men had failed? The longest lasted almost the entire time until a life-threatening injury had caused his extraction.

The news footage had been disturbing. The contestant was strapped to a stretcher and babbling incoherently as he was loaded into the ambulance. He had suffered multiple rib fractures, a concussion, and a shattered femur. They said he experienced a multi-story fall off the Ferris wheel. He was lucky to be alive.

The most recent death had occurred two years ago, on Valentine's Day. A woman was impaled on an ice sculpture. To this day, the circumstances surrounding her death remain unknown. Internet message boards still discussed theories.

The last Christmas event occurred in a wooded area. The 19-year-old didn't see a bear trap underneath the fresh layer of powdered snow. He tapped out immediately, but the damage was done. His ankle was shattered, and the skin was shredded. He required an amputation.

"The purpose of this experience is not to inflict lasting harm. When people act on impulse, addiction, poor decision-making, and maladaptive behaviors, injury and death are possible." He adjusted his glasses and slid a piece of paper across the desk. "All participants are required to sign a personal injury waiver."

She read the waiver carefully. It simply stated that The Society was not responsible for lasting injury or death. It was unnerving, but Tallulah signed it. Next was an additional waiver due to her lack of health insurance.

He nodded in affirmation. "You are allowed to defend yourself if you feel the situation calls for it."

"That's reassuring," she replied sarcastically.

He shuffled through the other papers, moving on.

"We received the results of your physical. The tests for STIs and communicable diseases were negative. All the actors were tested in kind."

It was confirmation that sexual contact was expected. Though Tallulah would never voice her dark fantasies aloud, the thought made her tingle. Sex and horror went hand in hand.

"Your safe word is 'rutabaga.' Say it, and you will be extracted immediately from the site, and the game will end. You must last the entire twelve hours to claim the prize money. We have your banking details. The sum will be transferred to you immediately after the siren sounds."

"And what if I'm incapacitated at any point?"

"In the event of a gag, you can use a nonverbal cue to signal distress. You will wear a tracking collar that is specifically designed to monitor heart rate, temperature, sleep cycles, and more. It has a trigger button that you may press to signal us immediately. An alarm is installed within the collar. It will vibrate every hour it is around your neck. If your hands are bound, knock five times against any surface."

"How will someone know?"

"There are over a hundred cameras placed throughout the fairgrounds. Your collar and the actors' masks have micro cameras and microphones to relay feedback to security. The actors know where the out-of-bounds limits are for your safety. Stick within them at all times. All actors are trained to step aside immediately in the event of extraction."

He pointed to the last few pages that required initials and signature. Her heart pounded as she scrawled across the final line of the NDA. All contestants signed a non-disclosure agreement with a steep penalty.

"Any other questions?" the man asked.

"Just one. Who is The Society?"

The man chuckled. "They are a group of individuals that enjoy their anonymity, Miss Daniels. Now, if you'll be so kind as to follow Nurse Roberts, we can get started. You need to be on the field in an hour."

A bubbly blonde in blue scrubs entered the room from a side door Tallulah hadn't realized was there.

"If you'd please follow me, Miss Daniels. I need to get a set of vitals before you're brought to wardrobe."

"Vitals?" Tallulah asked.

"Yes. First, we'll check your height and weight, followed by your basal body temperature, blood pressure, and pulse. We need a baseline before fitting your collar."

The women sat in a room hardly larger than a washroom. A digital blood pressure cuff squeezed Tallulah's upper arm. She opened her mouth to allow the nurse to stick a thermometer under her tongue.

"Temp 97.9. No fever. Your blood pressure is 110/69. Normal. Everything looks good on our end. Just one other question: When was your last menstrual period?"

"About two weeks ago?"

She handed Tallulah a bottle. "Here you go. Hydration is important. Once you're inside the park, you won't have the chance to eat or drink anything."

Tallulah's full pink lips stretched around the mouth of the bottle as she sipped the water under the watchful eyes of the nurse. They chatted for a few minutes while she finished drinking.

She became disoriented as the room around her spun. Her head was suddenly too heavy for her neck and lolled to the side. Tallulah's shoulders slumped, and she almost slipped from her chair.

"How are you feeling, Tallulah?"

The woman's voice became distant and unfamiliar, as if she were speaking underwater. Tallulah's tongue was too thick to respond. Instead of answering, she could only smack her lips in frustration.

"Good, Tallulah. Very good. They are going to love you. Your twelve hours will officially start when you enter the park. We'll see you upon your return."

CHAPTER 2

ENTERING THE PARK

A SIREN BLARED throughout the park and rattled around Tallulah's skull. She groaned and blinked at her pitch-black surroundings. Her head banged against a short ceiling as she attempted to sit up.

Tallulah reached her hands up and touched a solid wood plank. She felt around, and it didn't take long for cold realization to envelop her in dread. She quickly sobered as she realized she was completely naked and encased in a box.

"Help!" she screamed, beating her fists against the rough, wooden lid. "Can anyone hear me?"

Quickly, her breathing became shallow as she fought panic. Her vision went white as she kicked and pushed—anything to break free. She clawed at the lid as claustrophobia threatened to overtake her.

She wept and thought for the first time this was all a mistake. Tallulah had clearly been wrong in thinking she could handle all this. Being buried alive wasn't outlined in the contract.

But then, she remembered the form she'd hastily filled out.

Hobbies? *I love watching horror movies. I also enjoy playing puzzle games.*

She was a horror movie buff any time of the year. But there was just something special about watching them during the spooky season. She preferred the paranormal ones with demons and hauntings over slasher flicks or groups caught in some weird cult.

She always rolled her eyes because no one ever listened to the practical voice that wanted to get the fuck out of there. She'd fallen into that trap all on her own.

Fears? *Zombies, heights, serial killers, small spaces, being buried alive, and drowning.*

Fantasy? *I've always wondered how erotic being bitten by a vampire would be. I fantasize about spreading blood on my skin and fucking in lusty euphoria. I love the gothic aesthetic and dream about being debuted into The Society as a newborn vampiress.*

What a fucking idiot. She had given them the blueprint to her own terror. *Bravo*, she thought. This realization, however, failed to bring her comfort.

"HELP!" she screamed.

She forced herself to breathe. She needed to be rational in the face of fear. Surely they wouldn't actually kill her, *right*?

"Hello, Tallulah," a deep sultry voice greeted her from a speaker in the coffin she hadn't noticed before. "Your time has started. Don't forget your safe word. Otherwise, find the trigger and rise from the grave to play with us if you're brave enough."

It took a minute for his words to register. He'd said *trigger*. She felt around the padded lining along the sides until her fingers caught on a small seam. There was a handle beneath it she could pull with her finger. She'd been too panicked to notice it before.

Hinges creaked and groaned as they moved. Black soil that had been sitting on top shifted and began falling into the coffin. Tallulah barely had time to take a breath before she became engulfed.

Thankfully, it wasn't packed dirt; it was soft and fluffy like potting soil. She didn't have to drag herself more than a foot out of the shallow grave. She pushed up and attempted to spit the dirt from her lips. It tickled her nose, causing her to sneeze. Tallulah's hands were full of dirt, and she was unable to wipe her eyes, leaving her at a disadvantage without sight.

The same sultry voice she'd heard before spoke again. "Two feet to your right is a fountain where you can rinse off. I suggest you move quickly, as you aren't alone."

The hairs on the back of Tallulah's neck rose. She practically jumped the two feet and felt around. Her hands came in contact with cool stone, and the bubbling fountain was unmistakable. The water was ice cold, but she had no choice.

She rinsed her hands first, doing her best to ensure they were washed clean. Then she cupped her hands, letting the water pool before splashing her face. Tallulah wiped her lips and repeated the process several times before opening her eyes.

A groan caught Tallulah's attention. She stiffened and quickly looked over her shoulder and wished she hadn't. She bit back a scream as she watched a group of zombies eating flesh.

The grotesque creatures appeared in varying states of decay. Their skin was pallid and hung loose as though pounds of adipose tissue were lost. What remained of the naked female's hair was dirty to the point that its original color was indistinguishable.

It can't be real! Zombies aren't real! They're clearly actors who are eating something made to look like a human torso.

One of the zombies made a low guttural sound as it dug into a bloody chest cavity. Bones that were likely ribs cracked with a loud *snap*. The undead creature pulled out the bone and cleaned the muscle off with its teeth.

"You'd better move while they're busy feasting."

Tallulah was nauseated at the sight of entrails being removed. Blood splattered from an organ as a creature bit into it. Was it a liver or a kidney? She didn't know. She clamped a hand over her mouth to stifle a gasp.

"This can't be real," she said to the disembodied voice.

"Isn't it, though? I certainly wouldn't want to sit around and find out. Exit the cemetery and turn left. Run to the house of mirrors."

"Who are you?" she asked the disembodied voice.

"Move!" he shouted.

Their conversation had caught the attention of the undead. Dull, lifeless eyes fixated on her. Slowly and disjointedly, they moved like a herd in her direction—one step, then another. Tallulah glanced around, trying to find something with which to defend herself.

"Run, Tallulah!" the voice commanded. She wasn't going to stick around and be told again.

A shot rang out. She glanced over her shoulder and saw one of the zombies fall. Black ooze ran down the face of another undead before it fell to the ground. Several more deafening shots rang out disturbing the silence. Tallulah couldn't see the mysterious shooter but didn't wait to see what became of the remaining zombies.

As Tallulah ran, she came across a billboard that read *Stay and Play.* The image of a smiling little girl with pigtails had been altered to a demonic child with a sinister sneer. A tattered corner fluttered, being blown by a breeze that didn't exist in the still night.

Terror and excitement made Tallulah shiver with anticipation. She had already faced two of her biggest fears before the first hour ended as the collar around her neck buzzed. She wondered what lay in store for the other eleven.

CHAPTER 3
HOUSE OF MIRRORS

A WOODEN SIGN that read *House of Mirrors* crashed down before her. Tallulah hesitated, worried the entire structure might collapse. A chainsaw whirred to life in the shadows to the right of the building. A seven-foot-tall man with a hairy barrel chest and stained overalls stepped into the light. A burlap sack with a drawn scarecrow face covered his head as he wielded the loud, whining weapon.

Tallulah shrieked as he stepped closer to her. She took her chances and ran into the house of mirrors. Thankfully, the man gave up the chase the moment she crossed the threshold. It dawned on her that she was being corralled and needed to be cautious before she was blindly led into danger.

She didn't recognize herself in the mirrors. Her long dark hair was knotted and sticking out in wild directions. Mud caked her face and fair, naked skin.

She felt her way around and realized that even the entrance had disappeared behind the wall of mirrors. Tallulah's hazel eyes went wide as a phantom formed in the cloudy glass before her. She quickly glanced behind her, but there was no one there. She trembled as she felt the inhuman breath of the ghoul on her bare skin, leaving goosebumps in its wake.

Her eyes were trained on the mirror; she couldn't glance away if she tried. A phantom hand caressed her collar and moved lower, to her breast. She shuddered as her chest rose and fell. Tallulah bit back a moan as her nipple pebbled beneath the ghostly fingers. Another hand made its way up her inner thigh. The cold touches made her shiver while igniting a simmering fire in her belly.

This isn't right, she thought. But her body disagreed as her legs spread wider involuntarily. The phantasm wailed, and invisible hands turned rough and threw her forward against the glass. Her head bounced painfully, disorienting her. The mirrors went out of focus, and the ghostly phantom turned into a menacing shadow.

Black fumes billowed from its gaping maw. Tallulah's body was enveloped in fire as the smoke entered her mouth and nostrils. She struggled to breathe and choked as her throat and lungs burned.

The thick smoke battered her insides in what could only be described as an invasion. There was no escape. The vapor solidified into an ambiguous mass.

Pressure increased between her thighs, causing her engorged clit to throb painfully. Tallulah fell to her knees, gasping for breath. The violation continued as the black mass spread her inner walls. Her last conscious thought was wondering if she was simply hallucinating from lack of oxygen as the pain turned into prickles of dark pleasure.

Tallulah's brain remained foggy as she was carried out of the house of mirrors. She blinked up at the man carrying her, gazing into eyes that were ice cold, somewhere between blue and gray. His square jaw was tight while the dark stubble barely concealed his cleft chin. His large lips looked as though he could swallow her whole.

As they walked past a dilapidated wooden shack, the seriousness of Tallulah's situation dawned on her. She couldn't lose herself in a fantasy. However, she wanted nothing more than to snuggle further into his strong arms. Something about him radiated warmth and security.

"Are you an angel?" she asked.

He chuckled darkly and lowered his head. His whisper was barely audible, "No, my sweet."

"Who are you?"

"Lucien. Close your eyes and rest. You're going to need it."

"Lucien—" She lost consciousness again.

CHAPTER 4

CAROUSEL FROM HELL

Tallulah's head spun as she awoke from the most pleasant dream, only to be plunged back into her nightmare. She attempted to raise her hand to block the bright lights and found herself in thick red leather cuffs. A short set of links bound her hands together.

Floodlights pierced the darkness around her, allowing Tallulah to see everything for the first time since she had escaped her grave. As her eyes adjusted, the hellish carousel came into focus.

The stallions were armored, with glowing red eyes and smoke billowing from their snouts. Their heads moved up and down as they cantered around the circle. The proud golden lions shook their long, lustrous manes and roared. Their predatory eyes studied her as though she were a gazelle in the Serengeti, and if she didn't run fast enough, they'd feast on her.

Sea serpents swished their scaly tails as comfortable in the air as in the depths of the ocean. Large black dragons flapped their wings and breathed fireballs into a stack of hay bales, making them burn in a glorious blaze.

The bonfire licked across the sky, warming her from a distance. Tallulah scrambled to rise and run from the carousel beasts and the line of fire which threatened to trap and burn her. However, she tripped and was unable to catch herself due to the restraints. She scraped her knee and hip, scratched her palms, and bumped her head. Stars flashed before her eyes.

"Fuck!" she cried.

Hoots, hollers, and jeers floated around her. Three men came from one side of the carousel, and three more men circled around the other, trapping her between them. She scooched backward in an attempt to flee the masked men.

"Where do you think you're going, whore?" one of the masked men asked as she jumped on the carousel.

"I'll take my chances with the beasts," she yelled.

They laughed. Out of nowhere, spooky music blared through speakers, and the carousel began to spin. Two other men smoothly jumped on the moving platform. The closest man wearing a skeletal mask with deep black eye sockets whistled, and the horse behind Tallulah grabbed her hair with its teeth. She twitched against the powerful beast.

"Stay away, freaks!"

Her heart threatened to pound out of her chest as a sense of dread encroached on her. Her arms were restrained and a demonic horse had her hair in its teeth. None of that terrified her like the men who were slowly approaching. She didn't need to see their faces to know their intentions were to use and abuse her naked body.

"The slut has a voice," said the man in a horned mask.

"We'll see what you have to say while you're choking on my cock, lovely." A man with a rubber white mask with black eyes, nose, and mouth approached from the other side. The black cloth covered his neck and reached his bare shoulders.

The six men were of varying heights, from athletic to portly body types, hairy to dolphin smooth, and all colors of the rainbow. She tried to identify them by mask, but even that was impossible as the environment spun so quickly that she became lightheaded.

"Don't come any closer," she screamed.

Her heart beat wildly to invisible drums. Blood whooshed through her ears as hysteria bubbled in her throat. She could barely breathe as the world around her seemed to spin out of control.

The skeletal man, who appeared to be the gang leader, grabbed Tallulah's left ankle and shackled her with a chain. He straightened, meeting her eyes with his deep, dark sockets. She winced as he whistled sharply. The demonic stallion responded again by opening its powerful jaws to free her.

"The more you struggle, the harsher your punishment will be. I will set you free if you follow my directions." The black skeletal eyes looked down at her.

Tallulah realized it wasn't a mask; it had to have been some form of prosthetic makeup. His eye sockets were deep and black beneath a prominent brow bone, but her eyes were drawn to his open nasal cavity. His strong, well-defined jaw was lightly stubbled. It was beautiful, captivating, and freaky as hell. She longed to touch him to see what was real.

"Get on your knees like a good little slut."

Tallulah had a split second to decide if she would continue to fight or submit. Unfortunately, she couldn't see a way around the men, wild animals, and wall of fire. The skeletal leader had promised to set her free. How bad would it be if she wordlessly obeyed?

The man laughed. "Don't look so defeated. After I fuck your mouth, I'll remove your shackles, and we'll play cat and mouse. You can run, you can hide. But we will find you. And each time you're found, one of us will have his turn. Or we can all fuck you right here."

Her jaw dropped. She should be outraged, but the thought was thrilling. She'd always fantasized about being with multiple men. She wanted to be used for their pleasure.

"Here is good," she said wantonly.

The men roared in laughter.

"Oh, my boys, we truly have an accommodating fucking whore. You have a long way to go before earning our cocks." He put his hands on his hips and gazed at her. His eyes blazed from the empty sockets. "Open your mouth."

She did as instructed. He leaned close, and she wondered if he was going to kiss her, but instead, he pursed his lips and spat. She jerked back as it landed in her mouth. Human saliva was disgusting to her, and she moved to spit it out, but he grabbed her chin forcefully.

"No you don't. I own you tonight, little mouse. Every inch of your gorgeous body is mine. Now swallow."

She hesitated, and he clamped his hand over her mouth. "Swallow, little cunt. Playtime is over."

She had no choice and swallowed his warm saliva, gagging immediately. He let her go with a haughty grin.

CHAPTER 5
SKELETAL LEADER

Tears of humiliation rolled down Tallulah's cheeks as the men laughed at her.

The skeletal man undid his pants and pulled out the longest, thickest cock she'd ever seen. The veins pulsed proudly, but that wasn't what caught her attention. It was the magic cross that drew her wide-eyed stare. Then she noticed the six other piercings along the top of his shaft that looked like a corset.

"Have you never seen a man before, little mouse?" he asked as he stroked his cock.

"I... I have," she said weakly. "Just not... that."

"Open your mouth," he said before wagging his studded tongue.

Tallulah clamped her mouth shut and shook her head. His smug grin turned to fury in a second, and his backhand connected with her cheek.

"I'm going to make you my bitch and claim you in front of everyone. We will break you and enjoy ourselves."

He fisted her hair and pulled so hard she shrieked. While her mouth was open, he shoved his cock in without warning. She immediately began to fight the foreign invader, but he thrust himself deeper. The other hand wrapped around her throat and squeezed tightly.

She choked and looked up at him with wide, watering eyes. The corner of his lip lifted in a sneer.

"Just a bit more, little mouse. Punishment is necessary to show you your place."

Hoots and hollers from the other men were heard over the warped music, and the carousel spun faster and faster.

"Five..."

The cold steel of his jewelry was a sharp contrast to his hot rod.

"Four..."

Tallulah couldn't breathe, and this man didn't care.

"Three..."

Her eyes watered and rolled back into her head.

"Two..."

Darkness encroached on her vision as unconsciousness threatened to take her.

"One..."

The ball bearings scratched the roof of her mouth as he finally pulled back. Tallulah fell forward and sputtered and retched.

"The more you fight, the rougher we will be. Have you learned your lesson, or do you need another?"

"No," she replied hoarsely.

"Good, little mouse. Now, properly worship my cock. Spit on it, make it nice and sloppy."

She did as she was told. Tallulah closed her mouth and gathered her saliva, making her want to vomit. She spit on the tip as instructed. He guided her hand to the shaft, which was so thick she couldn't fully wrap her fingers around it. Her saliva served as lubrication to ease her movements.

The smoothness of him was interrupted by the studs. "Don't be afraid to tighten your fist and stroke. I love a firm hand."

He was right; she moved slowly because she was afraid of his piercings.

"Do you want to know how it will feel inside your pussy? My cock is studded for your pleasure. You will feel every inch of me buried deep inside you, stimulating nerves you never knew existed."

Tallulah's core clenched at his words. She was terrified and aroused simultaneously. She squeezed her thighs together, needing friction, and it didn't go unnoticed.

"Now lick the tip, slut. I want every bit of your hot mouth involved. I know you've never experienced the pleasure of a cock like mine. Before the night is over, you'll have your deepest desires fulfilled. But first, prove you're worthy."

His words hypnotized her. Her tongue flicked against his scorching skin. Once. Twice. She circled the four metal bearings around his head before kissing the slit where pre-cum beaded on the tip. His saltiness was refreshing and addictive.

Tallulah's sense of fear dissolved as she floated in a daze. She ignored the five men standing so close they could reach out and touch her if they chose. Instead, they watched her suck the pierced penis of the skeletal-faced man as if he were the most delicious lollipop. Small cooing sounds escaped her.

"You're a wonderful cocksucker. But it's time for me to fuck your face."

He grabbed her hair and moved her head forcefully back and forth, setting the pace and depth.

Tallulah closed her eyes, and he snapped. "Look at me while you're choking on my cum."

Her hazel eyes met his black gaze as his cock hit the back of her throat repeatedly. He grunted and growled, holding her against him as he unloaded so deep within her that she had no choice but to swallow his salty release or choke on it.

He pulled her to her feet and explored her body. His rough fingers pinched her nipples to stiff peaks. He twisted and watched as Tallulah's pleasured expression morphed into a grimace of pain.

He ran his finger through her lower lips, testing her wetness. She whimpered as he withdrew without penetration and ignored her needy clit.

"Look how wet you are, fucking slut. I practically raped your mouth, and you're soaking like a whore. Taste yourself from my finger."

Tallulah keenly sucked his finger into her mouth, tasting her sweetness. Once he was satisfied, he removed the cuffs from her wrists and the shackle from her ankle.

She rubbed her sore wrists and jumped as he spanked her hard.

"I'm honoring what I said before. Run, bitch. When we catch you, the real fun begins." He sidestepped. "You have a one-minute head start."

The fire that had flamed around them earlier was extinguished so she could run safely. She hopped from the carousel on unsteady legs and almost fell flat. The men watching her laughed. However, a handsome man in a masquerade mask reached his hand out to help steady Tallulah.

"Thank you," Tallulah said to the Prince before taking off.

"Tick tock," a hairy, barrel-chested man with an ape mask called after her.

CHAPTER 6
CORN MAZE

TALLULAH DIDN'T HAVE LONG, as the men continued their countdown behind her. Her heart beat the rhythm of every second that passed. She took a few precious seconds to look in both directions to find an avenue to run.

To the right was a game alley. Many of the stalls had fallen over. Red and white striped canopies were dull and gray with time and rot. It didn't look like she would be able to find an effective hiding spot with six pursuers.

To her left was a tall corn maze. The stalks were dry and withered and didn't look inviting. But the footpath was only wide enough to accommodate two walking shoulder-to-shoulder.

She decided to take her chances in the corn maze. The maze was dark, lacking the floodlights that lit up the grounds around the carousel.

Fond memories from childhood experiences gave way to adrenaline-fueled terror. She pushed herself as fast as her shaky legs and burning muscles could carry her. Occasionally, she glanced over her shoulder to ensure she was staying ahead of her hunters.

It proved to be a mistake as she missed a fallen stalk. Tallulah's foot caught, and she tumbled head over heels on the packed dirt.

"Fuck!" she cried, too loudly.

Realizing her mistake, she clapped a hand over her mouth. Her bare foot was scratched, and her ankle throbbed. She pushed herself backward off the path in an attempt to squeeze her lithe body between the proud corn stalks.

She willed her heart to quiet its relentless quivering. Though scared, Tallulah couldn't deny the thrill of being chased. A stark realization fell over her. She had again played right into the hands of those men. She was a willing mouse.

Stupid mouse, she chastised herself. Heavy footfalls plodded down the path, approaching her hiding spot. She closed her eyes, allowing her sense of hearing to sharpen in the darkness. She only heard one set of steps. When they paused in front of her hiding spot, Tallulah's eyes went wide.

The feet were encased in large tan work boots. Their owner grunted. "I know you're here, little slut," he called. "I can smell your fear."

He inhaled deeply and chuckled. "And I can smell your arousal."

His large hands split the stalks above her, and she screamed.

"Found you."

She hit as hard as she could, aiming right between the ape-masked man's legs. "Oof. You bitch!" She scrambled back through the corn wall and pulled herself to her feet.

"You can run, but you can't hide! When I find you, I'm going to drag you out of here by your neck."

Tallulah couldn't run with her twisted ankle but hobbled as quickly as possible. His heavy steps followed at a steady pace behind her. She hurried along until she came to a dead end.

With nowhere to go, Tallulah was determined not to surrender easily.

"Go through the wall to your right," the disembodied voice sounded in her ear again.

"Who are you?" she asked.

Ignoring her question, he replied, "Quickly!"

The large leaves tickled Tallulah's bare skin as she squeezed through the stalks. "Why do you keep helping me?" she asked.

"What makes you think I'm helping you? Maybe I'm leading you to me. Maybe I want to keep you for myself."

"Do you?" she asked.

"Maybe..." he replied. "Turn left."

He continued to guide her through the maze until she was on the other side.

"Thank you," she said sincerely.

"Don't thank me, Tallulah. You still have a lot of time left."

She hadn't thought about the time remaining. "I won't quit."

"Good girl. Now, quickly. He's closing in on you. Find someplace downwind to confuse his olfactory receptors."

Tallulah found herself in the food truck alley. She took a moment to catch her breath and observe her surroundings. There must've been a reason she was led here. The first stall she approached was a popcorn stand with moldy and stale food in the grimy window. A funnel cake cart with fryers full of old, dirty oil was right next to it.

A little further down, she came across a modern cooler with *Tallulah* written on it. She cautiously opened it and found a bottle of water. Her excitement at the find was short-lived as she recalled being drugged by the nurse.

"I promise it's safe to drink," Lucien assured her.

Tallulah twisted off the cap with joy and took a large gulp. The cold, refreshing liquid soothed the ache in her throat. She splashed a little of the cold water on her dirty hands. There was no way for her to carry the bottle, so she chugged the rest of it before moving on.

Thinking about her mysterious savior's words, she thought this might be a good place to rest for a moment. Tallulah hid inside one of the broken-down trucks with a lock inside. She grabbed a metal ladle and leaned her head against the wall.

At some point, she had dozed off. But the slightest sound had her twitching. She tightened her grip around the handle of the ladle until her knuckles became white.

CHAPTER 7
DEMON SPAWN

THE DOOR BUSTED IN, causing Tallulah to jerk awake.

"Found you, little mouse," the ape-man said.

"Stay back," she shrieked, brandishing her weapon.

He grabbed her by the ankle as she kicked and whacked him with the ladle. It didn't do anything but piss off the burly man. He flipped her over and took the ladle as easily as taking candy from a baby.

Tallulah bit her lip as he used it to spank her ass. Her attempt at restraint was no longer successful as he beat her in rapid succession. She sobbed at the blinding pain as the cold metal continued to connect with her skin.

She'd been spanked before by a partner. He had left pleasant tingles on her skin as part of foreplay, but it hadn't been dominance or punishment.

"Bitches need to learn their place." He hooted and grunted like an actual ape seconds before she felt liquid heat splash across her lower back and ass.

The ape hoisted her over his shoulder and carried her from the truck. They made their way back to the center of the fairgrounds. Tallulah kicked and screamed, beating his back with her fists. But a hard spank and firm grip on her ass brought her back in line.

He threw her to the ground. Her landing was so rough, she bit her tongue. The metallic taste of blood flowed down her throat. Before she could escape, a tall, athletic man in a horned mask dropped his knee on her neck. She lifted her hands to push him off, but he twisted, applying ample pressure to her airway. He pulled a knife and a blindfold from his pocket and ran the smooth side against her cheek.

"Don't squirm," he hissed.

He tied the blindfold, plunging her into pitch darkness. She heard whispers around her, speaking in tongues she couldn't understand. She wondered if there was an audience, though she hadn't seen one just moments ago.

The man alleviated Tallulah's struggle to breathe slightly by reducing pressure while keeping her pinned. The tip of his knife trailed down her chest. Though she tried her hardest not to squirm, it was impossible to remain still.

The horned demon pressed the tip harder against her skin, and immediately, a drop of scarlet blood swelled under the edge of the knife. She howled in pain as he dragged it an inch across her chest. Warm blood trickled from the shallow slice.

"I want you to see me now," he hissed, pulling the blindfold away.

He made a show of licking her blood off the blade's sharp edge. Tallulah gasped as he flicked his bloody tongue at her. He laughed maniacally and didn't seem to feel any pain from the masochistic act. The demon licked the valley between Tallulah's breasts, letting the blood from his tongue mix with her own.

He twisted his knee, digging painfully into her throat. Her vision went dark as her eyes rolled back into her head. He moved off her and slapped her back to consciousness before straddling her chest.

"Wake up, whore. I want you present while I have my fun with you."

He freed his long cock from the confines of his pants. The cold steel of the knife made another cut above her left breast, bringing Tallulah back to her senses. Her nipples hardened against her will as he teased them with the tip of the blade.

"I knew you were a freak like me. You have gorgeous round tits. I want to fuck them and have you wear my cum and blood."

He slicked his dick with their mixed blood before grinding between her breasts. His grip on her flesh was painful. Powerful thrusts against her chest encouraged blood to continue seeping from her wounds. He lowered his head and spit bloody saliva on his cock head for extra lubrication.

His hips snapped faster and faster. His face warped, showing the carnal beast's malevolent spirit. The whispers from an invisible audience grew louder. Tallulah flinched as the demon pressed the knife against her cheek again.

"Beg for my cum, like the needy slut you are. I'm going to paint you like a masterpiece."

"Please," she said.

He ground harder. "That's not good enough."

He brought the knife to the tip of his cock and pricked it. Warm blood dribbled against Tallulah's skin, awakening her primal desire. While the sickeningly dry, sweet metallic scent of blood mixed with sweat intoxicated her.

"Yes, please. Please! Give me your cum. Paint my tits with it." Tallulah lifted her hands to her breasts and pushed them together.

His dark eyes lit up. "That's better."

He grabbed her hand and guided it to his cock. With his fist tight around hers, it was only a few strokes before he was pulsing against her palm.

"Open your mouth," he commanded.

She opened for him just before the first hot jet landed on her tongue. The next hit her chin. He pumped the remainder onto her chest. She was a sticky, disgusting mess by the time he was finished.

"What a good little slut you are."

Humiliation enveloped Tallulah like a cold blanket as the demon took his weight and warmth away. She was exposed and vulnerable as a thousand stars witnessed their exchange.

If she ran, the demon would certainly give chase. He slapped her cheek before digging his claws into her body once more. His voice was like a knife in her ear.

"You are nothing," he said. "You are weak and pathetic. You deserve to be punished."

Tallulah tried to block out his words, but it was useless.

The demon's claws dug deeper into her flesh, and Tallulah cried out in pain. "Please," she begged. "Don't do this."

His laughter was a cruel, mocking sound. "You are nothing," he said again. "You have no power to stop me."

Tallulah felt like she was going to die. The pain was unbearable, and the shame was overwhelming. She closed her eyes and waited for the end. She waited to feel that cold steel run across her neck.

But the end never came. Instead, she felt the demon's claws release her, and she opened her eyes to see him standing over her, his face twisted with rage.

“The night isn’t over yet,” he said.

He spat on her and was gone a moment later. Tallulah lay there for a long time, too afraid to move.

CHAPTER 8
FERRIS WHEEL

Despondent and alone, Tallulah was unsure how much longer she had to remain in hell. She was exhausted from her masked tormentors' repeated abuse and continuous chase.

"You're doing wonderfully, Tallulah. Only a little longer. The sun will rise soon." His words gave her hope. "Think of your prize and the financial independence you will gain through this experience."

She honestly hadn't thought of the money once since she'd woken in the grave. In theory, it seemed so easy when no real stakes were involved. But now, it was a matter of survival. The prize money was the least of her worries.

Financial independence was hard won in this twisted game. Every inch of her body and willpower were being pushed to their limits. Would it be worth it if she couldn't face herself in the mirror afterward? What about recurrent nightmares from trauma?

Was it the drugs or her own fear that caused hallucinations? Reality blurred around her, and it had never been so appealing. Would any future experience offer her the same thrill?

"That's right, my sweet. Embrace the chaos."

"Where are you, Lucien?" she asked.

"The most ruthless of the group is on your trail. Run!" he shouted, ignoring her question.

Tallulah hesitated. "Where?"

She looked around for a clear path as a Viking horn sounded in the distance. She faced unknown peril, but nowhere Lucien had led her to that point had been safe.

She wanted to believe him. There was an inexplicable connection. But was he a savior or villain? What if he was there to torture her psychologically? He was the horror movie hero who convinced the heroine he was a good guy who stabbed himself to throw suspicion off. In the third act, he reveals himself as the bad guy, and she would be sorry if she didn't kill him.

What if he was genuine? He'd carried her ever so tenderly from the house of broken mirrors. The man in the royal mask, her prince. The man who'd lent a hand when she stumbled off the carousel.

Following the prince's advice, her feet found a flight of their own volition. Eventually, she came to a tall chain-link fence. Laughter bubbled from her chest as she realized it was the perimeter of the fairgrounds. It was surreal, seeing that the walls of her prison weren't walls at all. Anyone could scale the tall fence in or out.

Tallulah wrapped her fingers around the wire. The metal clinked as her body involuntarily sagged against it.

The alarming low mournful wail of a war horn sounded somewhere behind her, signaling it was time for the kill. It reverberated through her skull. She wanted to cower and cover her ears. Instead, she moved, intending to scale the fence.

"If you leave the boundary, it is an automatic forfeit."

Somehow, she knew she was the only one who could hear Lucien. It was as if he spoke directly using telepathy. *That's not possible,* she thought.

"And yet, that's exactly what's happening," he purred seductively. "You need to move, Tallulah. When you touched the fence, a perimeter alarm was triggered. Your location was compromised. Run west toward the Ferris wheel. If you make it to the warehouse, you can hide until your time runs out."

"I can't," she cried. "I can't do this anymore. I'm sorry."

She returned her attention to the fence. Where would she go? What would she do? Returning to the life she had before didn't seem possible anymore.

"You are so close. I promise to come for you. Just wait for me in the warehouse. Now run!"

Tallulah gathered the strength she no longer had and ran. As the Ferris wheel came into view, Tallulah was amazed it remained standing. Several pods were missing. Snapped cables dangled freely, and the axle appeared cracked. The enormous structure leaned menacingly. One strong gust of wind seemed enough to topple the entire thing.

She turned away and focused on the warehouse—approximately 100 yards away. A wolf-whistle caught her attention from the lower deck of the Ferris Wheel.

The structure groaned, and a spoke broke free, plummeting to the ground. It landed a foot in front of her. It was followed in rapid succession by half a dozen other spokes. They blocked her path and allowed the ghost-faced man to catch her.

“Where do you think you're going?” he asked in a raspy voice as though he’d smoked for hundreds of years.

He moved swiftly, causing Tallulah to fall to her knees. He grasped the ring around her neck and tugged. “I love a girl on her knees. But I have other plans first.”

He grabbed her hair and twisted it in his fist. “Follow me.”

Tallulah had no choice but to follow the ghost-faced man. He yanked so hard that a clump of hair tore from the roots, leaving her scalp on fire. She bit her lip to keep from screaming.

“I’m sorry, Tallulah,” Lucien said. “Wait for me. I'll find you no matter what.”

Instead of providing comfort, his words were an ice bath to her tortured soul. She felt numb and empty inside, like all the hope and warmth had been sucked out of her. Tears welled in her eyes, and her knees became weak. For the first time, Tallulah felt like she was in actual danger.

“The collar in your neck tracks your vitals. If they detect an arrest, you will be extracted immediately. You have your safe word. Don't be afraid to use it if you need to.”

Tallulah steeled her resolve. She wasn't going to quit. She was so close to achieving her goal that she could taste it. The hellish night was testing her strength of character, but she would prove unbroken.

The ghost-faced man dragged her to the base of the Ferris Wheel. He threw her to the ground and laughed.

"I like my prey to show some fight. You're just pathetic. Let's see if we can wake you up."

He kicked her hard enough that it knocked the wind out of her. Tallulah planted her palms on the ground as she sputtered and tried to push herself up.

But he climbed over her back and wrapped his forearm around her throat. He pulled her back against his chest and increased the pressure. His clothed erection dug into her lower back, making her feel his excitement.

"Fight back," he growled.

Tallulah clawed at his bare arms, digging her nails in so deep they broke skin, but he didn't relent. She fought like hell and attempted to elbow him, but his sleeper hold deprived her brain of the necessary oxygen to allow her muscles to move. His laughter in her ear was the last thing she heard as her body went limp like a rag doll.

CHAPTER 9
KALEIDOSCOPE

A SCRATCHY, stiff material covered Tallulah's head and face when she came to. She moved her hands only to find herself bound again, this time with what felt like cables from the Ferris wheel.

Tallulah struggled against her bonds but was unable to move due to the tight coils. She was spread-eagled with the cold, rough concrete scraping her back.

"Hello?" she whispered. "Lucien—"

Freezing water was poured over Tallulah's head. It caused the burlap sack over her face to stick to her nose and mouth. She spluttered, unable to breathe. The water continued to pour over her, filling her mouth and nose.

Yet another of her greatest fears was becoming a living nightmare. She was being tortured, and for what? Her knuckles turned white from clenching her fists tightly.

Lucien! Save me!

Her heart sank when he didn't answer. Tallulah couldn't think, breathe, or scream. She thrashed like a trapped wild animal, but there was no escape.

The water slowed to a trickle. She immediately turned her head to the side and inhaled blessed oxygen through her mouth. Almost as soon as the torture had stopped, someone grabbed her clothed head and turned her back again.

This time, instead of being simply doused with water, she felt a man's penis between her spread legs. She gasped as he drove in to the hilt. His enormous size split her apart as she was drowning.

The safe word she was assigned was completely forgotten. For a moment, she couldn't remember her own name. Terror and trauma twisted her into someone unrecognizable.

She floated outside herself. The ghost-faced man was inside her, pumping fiercely, disregarding her needs or desires. Her body betrayed her, becoming slick, allowing him to slip in and out faster and harder.

Every bit of her body was on fire. The pain was so intense that her brain disengaged. The water flow was stopped again, and the mask was removed from her face. She sobbed as she gasped for air.

The black and white of his face swam in her vision. Behind him stood four others in black masks with neon tubes. Pink, purple, green, and blue colors swirled in a kaleidoscope of twisted beauty. In Tallulah's delusion, she beckoned them forward. The glowing hues danced before her.

The pink eyes were open with a wide smile that she returned through watery eyes. The blue man was cross-eyed and frowned as he tilted his head one way and then the other. The green and purple men's expressions continued to change.

"Please stop," she cried.

Ghost face howled in pleasure. "Your pussy is so fucking tight. We're not going to stop until every hole of yours is filled with cock and cum."

His hips snapped faster, becoming aggressive. He pulled out and spit on her naked mound and rubbed the tip of his cock in it before plunging back in. He lifted her hips, changing the angle and hitting a spot inside her that lit up her core.

He continued moving as each of the other four men untied a limb. Tallulah sagged in relief.

"You made it so fucking easy for us. I think you enjoy being fucked by big cocks."

The blue masked man dropped next to her face. He exposed his large black cock. He took himself in hand and tapped her cheeks with it. "Do you enjoy being owned, little slut?"

One of the other men grabbed a cable and tied it to the collar around her neck. They turned her over and forced her onto all fours like an animal.

"Bark for us like the bitch you are," the man in green said.

Her lips remained clamped until a hard hand came down on her ass.

"Arf, arf," she whined.

"Bitches like you were made to submit."

"Good girl. You deserve a treat."

The tip of a cock brushed against her ass crack. The man spread her cheeks and spit on her bud. She tried to wiggle away in a vain attempt to stop him from using her virgin hole.

A man on each side grabbed her under the arms to hold her steady for the one at her backside.

"You belong to us."

"Scream for us," the man against her back whispered in her ear before pushing inside her.

"Ahhh!" she screamed.

He didn't prep her, didn't use care. His thick cock tore her ass open with a pain that was unlike any other. He pushed through her barrier and fought her resistance, not stopping until his hips met hers.

Tallulah felt as though she would choke. He leaned over her, and she collapsed under his weight. His hot breath burned the bare skin on her shoulder.

Her ring tightened around his shaft as he attempted to withdraw. Tallulah willed her body to relax to ease the pain. He wouldn't slow down or stop because it hurt. Instead, her body tensed further as he slapped her ass. She felt every inch of the pierced cock inside her. Every movement of his shaft stimulated nerves that made her quiver.

He grabbed her hips and forced her ass up higher to change the angle. She sobbed as he slapped her hard again. He spread her cheeks apart and watched as his dick moved in and out of Tallulah's body.

"I love breaking in sluts and showing them their place."

He spit on the sore hole again and plunged back in. She screamed as he bottomed out within her. He was deliberately slow with every withdrawal, letting her feel every piece of his metal corset.

Tallulah moaned as the pain became pleasurable. The stimulation was surreal. The two men kept her pinned down while the man fucking her ass increased intensity.

Tallulah panted and broke into a sweat even though she was freezing in the cool night air. Groans and grunts came from the man pistoning in and out of her sore ass. Her engorged clit begged for attention as wetness seeped down her thighs.

"Come for me, whore," the man fucking her ass commanded.

He reached beneath Tallulah's body and flicked her clit before pinching it. Her core tightened as he plunged himself as deep as he could. She howled with release as unexpected ecstasy overwhelmed her. She was swallowed by the waves as heat tore through her.

"What a good little slut you are. You came from being fucked in the ass."

She collapsed against the men holding her. Aftershocks coursed through Tallulah as he slowly withdrew. A surprising emptiness overwhelmed her.

"We have plenty of time to fuck every hole of yours raw."

CHAPTER 10
MASKED MEN

"YOUR GAPING HOLE IS A VISION."

The man in the green mask pulled the cable tied to the collar around Tallulah's neck. Her body jerked forward, bumping into his stomach. One hand held her tight to him, and the other pulled his pants down.

His penis was thinner and longer than the rest in juxtaposition to his short and wide body. He tapped her lips with the tip, leaving a hint of his saltiness on her.

"Open up. Suck me deep and keep it sweet."

Something inside Tallulah snapped. Her desire to resist could no longer be found. Knowing that Lucien didn't come for her when she needed him the most broke her. Subservience was the only way through. Maybe they would grant her wish of death afterward.

As the cock slipped further into her mouth, she swirled her tongue against the pulsating veins. Letting herself go was freeing. She could even say *pleasant*.

After facing her deepest fears, she was now willing to allow herself to fulfill one of her darkest fantasies by allowing anonymous strangers to take her in dirty and depraved ways. Why had she resisted them so long?

Soft humming met her ears. It took Tallulah a minute to realize that it was her wanton purring. The man before her swept her hair aside. She looked up at the neon colors and wondered what color his eyes were.

He thrust his hips and held her there as she attempted to swallow to ease the gagging sensation. It only succeeded in allowing him to slip further into her throat until her nose hit his abdomen.

"Good little mouse."

His praise sent a jolt of pleasure to Tallulah's core, stoking a fire in her belly. He withdrew and laid down on the concrete. She was captivated by the slow, confident way he stroked himself.

"We're waiting to play," someone said as they shoved her from behind. "Sit on him."

Slut... Whore... Mouse... They reinforced that she was no longer Tallulah Daniels. She wasn't a person; she was their plaything. This was the point of no return.

There was no preamble, no foreplay. Two men helped Tallulah settle reverse cowgirl on the man's lap. She slowly sank onto him. The difference in the size of his penis to the pierced one that claimed her virgin ass first was staggering. He was thinner and able to push through her relaxed ring with less resistance, but his length impaled her.

"Lean back," he said, wrapping his arms around her chest.

With her feet planted on the ground and her back against the chest of the man beneath her, the remainder of Tallulah's body was fully exposed. Tallulah felt embarrassed as she saw four other men, naked except for their masks, which had changed again.

They were all in masquerade masks like her prince wore. Tallulah was disappointed that Lucien wasn't among them, while at the same time thankful he didn't see her being fucked by the other men.

The only one she recognized was the man with the pierced cock. He wore a golden metal wolf-like mask. He had been the first to take her mouth, then her ass. He was clearly the leader of this gang, as they all waited for his order.

His penis wasn't the only part of him that was decorated with metal. His nipples were pierced with horizontal bars, and both his nostrils and septum had silver hoops.

He flicked his studded tongue before spitting onto Tallulah's bare mound. He spread the warm saliva between her folds with the fat head of his cock.

"Moan for me," his hoarse voice said.

Tallulah didn't need to fake it as he ground against her clit before pushing inside her with a single stroke. The men stole her breath as she was stretched and filled. The man in her ass remained still while the one in her pussy moved in and out. He rubbed against the thin barrier separating the two of them, and amazing wasn't enough to describe how sensitive and raw the experience was.

The metal ridges on his penis rubbed against her secret spot, making her hornier than she'd ever felt. Tallulah moved her hips to meet his as they grew hotter. She squirmed and whimpered as he pounded in and out of her pussy.

"Will one of you assholes shut her the fuck up?" he growled.

He wrapped his hand around her throat and shoved three fingers into her mouth in punishment. He snapped his hips faster, owning her completely. Still, Tallulah found enjoyment in the act. The man beneath her pinched her nipples, which had become pouty from lack of attention. Her moans grew louder despite their efforts to kowtow her.

A man wearing a black and gold Venetian jolly mask that jingled as he moved thrust his meaty cock in her face. Another man in a black and silver horn-rimmed warrior mask looked like a supervillain as he approached. He grabbed her hair and stuck his cut dick against her cheek.

They took turns fucking her mouth. Left and right, her head bobbed. The jolly man moved hard and fast, while the warrior was slower, but no less harsh.

The leader of the men grunted and thrust deep, searing her insides with his hot seed. He humped against her hips, once... twice... and pulled out.

"Have at her, boys," he said.

He was replaced by the last man that she couldn't see. At that point, it didn't matter anymore. Tallulah fell into a deep well of pleasure thriving to escape as she gave herself over to their desires.

"Come for me, slut," the man commanded as he pinched her clit.

The overload of sensation hit her at once. Hands and cocks moved in tandem to use her for their pleasure, but granting her release was a gift. She became hyperaware of her lust boiling until white heat exploded within her.

Her core tightened and spasmed around the cocks in her ass and pussy. She lost the rhythm around the man in her mouth. Control was theirs, and ecstasy held her hostage.

Did it last seconds, days, years? The men took turns like she was the merry-go-round they had been riding.

"Please... please..." she begged.

"You want our cum, slut? We'll bathe you in it."

She didn't want it. She *needed* it.

CHAPTER 11
PRINCE

A SIREN SOUNDED in the distance, dragging Tallulah from the fog.

"Hello, little mouse." Lucien's sultry voice greeted Tallulah like a caress.

Tallulah's body lay broken and battered as she blinked up at her prince. He removed the black masquerade mask to expose his handsome face. His gray eyes were a perfect accompaniment to his caramel skin. His left brow was marred with a scar that she was tempted to run her finger across, but she didn't have the strength to raise her arm.

Her heart pounded in her chest. Not from fear, but something else. Was it simply an attraction to this man or something more?

"Lucien—" Her voice was a hoarse whisper. "I waited for you."

"Shh!" He touched her cheek. "Don't waste your strength."

Lucien's smile made Tallulah swoon. He gathered her in his strong arms and lifted her bridal style. She snuggled against his tattooed chest. The words *Strength Through Loyalty* took up residence across his collar. An enormous horned skull was centered with his nipples in the dark eye sockets.

The tattoos on his strong arms were visual depictions of heaven on one side and hell on the other. She heard the choir of angels sing while the eternally damned screamed in torment.

"You're beautiful," she sighed.

He chuckled lightly.

"You wouldn't say that if you knew me."

"I do know you," she said with a wince and blacked out.

TALLULAH AWOKE FLOATING ON A CLOUD. Lucien smiled at her with a gleaming grin. One sharp tooth poked over his lower lip.

"You're the sexiest vampire I've ever seen." She giggled.

"I'm your vampire, little mouse." He winked. "Watching you through the trials excited me. I'm proud of you."

Lucien's words wrapped her in warmth as much as his strong arms. He was home.

"Make love to me, my prince."

"You're insatiable. Haven't you had enough tonight?" He chuckled.

"I'm hungry for you."

“Oh, little mouse, I crave you.” His gray eyes clouded with desire.

She squealed as he pounced on her. “I’ve missed you.”

He gently brushed her cheek and pushed her hair behind her ear.

“I’m here now.”

“Please make love to me,” she begged.

Lucien closed his eyes and sighed. “It’s dangerous, given the state your physical body is in.”

“This isn't real, is it?” She frowned.

Lucien ran his thumb across her quivering lower lip. She chased it with her tongue and sucked the tip in. He probed her mouth for a moment.

“What do you think this is?” he retorted.

She shook her head. The truth was apparent, but more than anything, she was willing to indulge her subconscious.

“I don’t care. I ache for you.”

“How can I say no to you?”

Tallulah spread her legs wantonly. She quirked her finger, enticing him. His eyes slowly perused her body, making her squirm. She caressed her fevered skin, stopping to squeeze her breasts and tweak her nipples.

“Yes,” he hissed. “Show me where you want me.”

She trailed her hand down her body until she reached the apex between her thighs. Tallulah spread herself open for Lucien’s gaze as she circled her clit with her fingers. Her breath quickened as she pleasured herself before her captive audience.

"That's enough," he said. "It's my turn now."

Lucien vaulted over her. He lowered his lips to hers in a passionate kiss. His tongue met hers in a tango. She wrapped her arms around his broad shoulders and clung to him, pressing her chest against his.

Tallulah lowered her hand to grasp Lucien's throbbing member, but he stopped her.

"Slow down," he said against her lips as she pouted. "I want a taste first."

Lucien kissed down her neck, leaving love bites along the way. He nibbled, sucked, kissed, and soothed every spot with his tongue. When he lingered on her breasts, he wrapped his arm around her, causing her back to arch so he could suckle her nipple.

He kissed her soft belly and licked around her navel, dipping his tongue in her belly button. She squirmed and giggled because it tickled.

"If you're laughing, clearly I'm not doing a good job."

Lucien split her lower lips with his hand and dove right in with long licks between her folds. Her engorged clit beckoned him closer, but he ignored it. He slipped a finger inside her tight channel.

"I need more," she whined.

"I love when my little mouse proves what a needy little slut she is. Beg for it, gorgeous."

"Please, Lucien. Please let me come."

"Almost."

He withdrew his finger and held it up before her. Tallulah eagerly sucked it into her mouth, tasting herself on his caramel skin.

"Your tongue is magical," he groaned as she swirled around his finger. "Would you like your reward?"

"Yes, sir," she whimpered.

He lowered his head again, this time paying homage to her clit. He sucked her pulsing desire into his mouth, and she bucked and cried.

"Scream for me," he said, flashing his pearly white fangs.

Tallulah obeyed and howled, coming like a freight train as he pierced her nub. He sucked her blood as she writhed and thrashed. He wrapped his arms around her hips to hold her steady.

Lucien released her clit and moved to her dripping slit to enjoy the juices she squirted.

"Naughty mouse. You soaked everything."

She giggled, still trying to catch her breath. "You brought it out of me."

"I hope you aren't finished yet."

"Never."

He smiled and licked the blood from his lip. Lucien bit his tongue with his fang and let the blood pool before kissing Tallulah. He transferred his blood to her, and she eagerly swallowed.

She was so desperate to feel Lucien, so ready. As he drove into her, her head fell back with a cry. She spread her legs wider, trying to take him as deep as she could. There was a space within her that only he could fill.

Though she was wet and well-prepped, he still stretched her to the point where pleasure met pain.

"Your pussy is so delicious. It weeps for me."

"Yes," she moaned as he thrust into her.

He was gentle only a moment for her to accept him within her. His movements became fast and furious as he loved her deeply and hard.

With eyes darkening like a thunderstorm and his handsome features twisting into a monstrous guise, he slammed his hips into Tallulah's. He lifted one of her legs over his shoulder to push deeper. He gripped Tallulah's wrists in his hand and held them over her head.

"Take me," he growled.

"Yes!" she cried.

Their slapping flesh met relentlessly until he roared his release. Before Tallulah's cries subsided, Lucien's fangs descended into her tender throat.

Tallulah screamed and convulsed as he swallowed her blood.

"I know it hurts, love. Just hold on. Come back to me, Sadie."

She didn't know who Sadie was, but something about the name resonated within her.

Tallulah's eyelids fluttered. Lucien's face swam before her, making her dizzy.

"Stay awake."

He shook her gently, causing her to groan.

"Did I win?" she asked.

"Shhh. Don't worry about the trials right now."

Lucien's voice soothed every ache she had. Somewhere, the lines between their realities became blurred. It wasn't a game as the lovers clung to one another.

"You have a choice to make, my tulip. Accept the prize money, and I can remove the burden of your memories. Or remain cognizant and accept the next invitation."

Before Tallulah could make a choice, she fell unconscious in his arms.

THE VICTOR

TALLULAH SAT in a parlor on a crimson crushed velvet loveseat. She was dressed in a black and red gothic ball gown with a sweetheart neckline and cascading ruffles. The taffeta was cool on her freshly healed skin.

A hair and makeup artist gave her smoky eyes and twisted her dark hair back, leaving ringlets around her face. She felt like a princess sitting with her hands crossed thoughtfully in her lap. Breathing was a habit that was no longer painful.

Tallulah's life was divided into two parts: before and after. *Before* was several failed relationships where she was left heartbroken. She'd never known her father, as he had passed away prior to her birth. *Before* was losing her mother after years of battling disease. Medical bills had mounted to crippling debt.

Working three jobs left her little time for socializing and dating. She found solace and enjoyment in watching horror movies and writing on online message boards. In retrospect, she suspected that was how she had come onto The Society's radar.

A fever dream left her in the *after.* Tallulah Daniels was among the few who had accepted an invitation from The Society and passed the trial. Many times she questioned what was real during her night in the fairground.

The news continued to share the story regarding the terror at the fair. Drone footage showed the mutilated corpses of several scare actors hidden beneath clothes stained with blood. Though she'd seen it many times and been questioned by authorities, Tallulah couldn't recount the events of the night.

Lucien's footsteps were so light she didn't hear him enter the room. The hair on the back of her neck stood up as he cleared his throat. He was breathtaking in his black brocade Victorian-style tailcoat and black trousers with a blood-red shirt. It wasn't lost on the young woman that their attire matched.

"Sadie?"

He spoke so softly and intimately that she became enraged. A torrent of emotions overwhelmed her at his proximity. She screeched and flew into him, beating his chest with her fists.

"How could you let me forget who I really am? How could you put me through all of this? Did you do all this to punish me?"

Lucien wrapped his arms around Tallulah and held her steady against his muscular chest as she sobbed against his shoulder.

"I love you. I love you so fucking much that it killed me to have you enter the trial. There's a reason I was on the ground and trying to help you."

Her heart fluttered at his confession. He loved her.

"Aren't you always part of it?"

He shook his head and said with a sigh, "Members of The Society are prohibited from participating in the events."

Tallulah's head and heart were conflicted. Her head was a foggy, fucked-up mess from her experiences and discovering a past they had shared. The treacherous organ in her chest had no doubts about Lucien's claims. Her heart carried him inside.

"What's next?" she asked.

"I love you so much that I'm ready to burn down The Society to be with you."

Tallulah lifted her chin to look into his eyes. Every word was laced with sincerity.

"And what if my memories never return?"

"We have a lifetime to make new ones."

THE TWISTED SOCIETY

Congratulations on surviving Scream at the Fair.

The Society invites you to be our guest of honor at an introductory dinner. A new set of trials will await you.

Are you ready?

THE TWISTED SOCIETY PRESENTS

The Winter Maiden

Sadie Winters was born into submission. She was expected to remain in the shadows, unseen and unheard, until her curious nature led to a chance encounter with one of her masters.

Cain, the eldest son of a Society member, became enthralled with the maiden and locked her away in his chambers to serve his every whim. With death willing to grant her freedom, Sadie was ready to embrace it with open arms until she met Lucien.

A forbidden love affair erupts between captive and master, leaving Sadie caught between brothers. When The Society discovers the truth, it becomes a race for survival in a game with no winners.

SONGS INSPIRED BY THE SEASON

Sweet Dreams (Are Made of This) - Marilyn Manson

This is Halloween - Marilyn Manson

Devil - Shinedown

Sound of Madness - Shinedown

Living Dead Girl - Rob Zombie

Love Bites (So Do I) - Hailstorm

Blood - In This Moment

Fully Alive - Flyleaf

Voodoo - Godsmack

Nothing Else Matters - Apocalyptica

Make Me Bad - Korn

Falling Away From Me - Korn

Halo - Soil

SONGS INSPIRED BY THE SEASON

Down with the Sickness - Disturbed

Happy? - Mudvayne

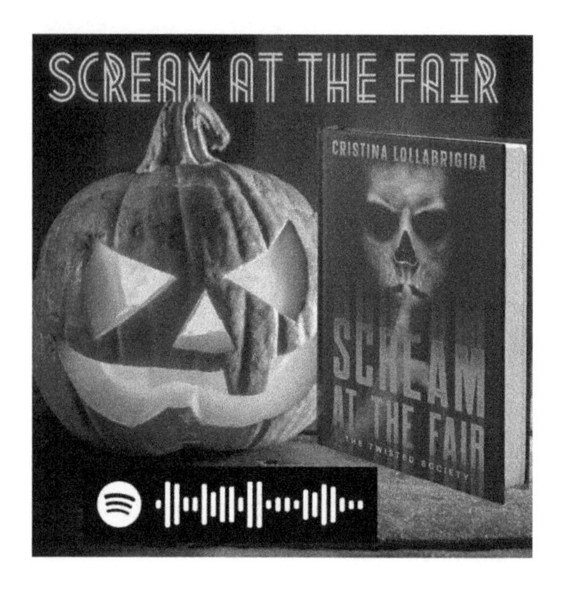

AUTHOR'S NOTE

This story was inspired by an insidious nightmare I had one night. I was asleep on my couch, and outside my window, an evil spirit was watching me. His grotesque face was mask-like and terrifying. Thankfully, the protective barrier around my home kept him from entering. When I entered the bathroom, I saw his reflection in the mirror.

I was taught that prayer in dreams such as these is powerful. I stuttered through the Our Father in my terror. It worked as it was meant to. I was able to wake myself up.

Unfortunately, I was unable to fall back to sleep. Adrenaline and fear kept me up until dawn. But I used the time productively. I wrote the first 600 words and description, put up the pre-order, and ordered the cover.

ABOUT THE AUTHOR

Cristina Lollabrigida is a romance lover who has always aspired to be a writer. She began her writing journey in grade school, but it wasn't until 2020 that she was inspired to write serialized works on an interactive story app.

Cristina is a multi-genre author. She writes steamy contemporary, spicy dark, and paranormal romances.

Originally from Chicago, Cristina is a country girl at heart and lived in rural Wisconsin for several years. She currently lives with her husband and their three children in South Carolina. Fall is her favorite time of year. And when she's not writing, she's reading.

ALSO BY CRISTINA LOLLABRIGIDA

Dark Romances

Accidental Bride

Upholding the law was all Drake Walker ever wanted to do. Until he found himself married to the one person that could ruin him...

Alessandra Russo.

Daughter of the notorious mafia Don.

Sheltered member of Chicago's elite.

Pawn.

She knows her life was never her own.

Hidden.

Abused.

Unloved.

The day her father announced she was to be wed to a stranger, she only hoped her unknown husband would save her from her dark and deprived life.

Now married to the city's top prosecutor, and the lead lawyer on the case against her brother, Alessandra finds herself in the balance of saving herself and saving her family. Relying on her training to meet her husband's deepest desires, she vows to do what she can to keep her unwilling husband happy, and both of them alive.

Marriage by Trial

Tired of being used as a pawn in everyone's plan, Alessandra decides it's time to take her future in her own hands, even if it means burning down the world around her.

Pawn.

That's all sheltered mafia princess Alessandra Russo will ever be.

She learned early on that all she was good for was pleasing men; both in and out of the bedroom.

That's how she was raised.

That's how she was trained.

After her arranged marriage to disgraced prosecutor Drake Walker, she had a taste of what a marriage with love could be like. Not just because she knows how to appeal to his darkest desires, but because, for once, she found someone who truly loves her for who she is.

With her happiness and marriage at risk, she must navigate being caught between rival mafia families to save the lives of everyone she has ever known.

The clock is ticking. She needs to decide if she can sacrifice her family for her one shot at love.

You're My Always

To have, to hold, and to protect... Always.

Officer Michael Miller took an oath to serve and protect, but his wife's disappearance on their first anniversary continues to haunt him.

Angela is the captive of a motorcycle gang leader. Recurring dreams of love with a handsome stranger ignite hope and her fighting spirit. She feels a soul-deep connection even though she doesn't know his name.

When Michael receives a plea for help he can't ignore, he seizes the opportunity to be the hero he failed to be. He finds backup in the most unlikely sources as he walks a fine line between revenge and justice.

Contemporary Romances

Running After You

Cinnamon Roll Hero (sin-a-mon roll he-ro): (n) a hero who is too sweet for this world...but will fight to the death for the people they care about

Join twenty of your favorite romance authors on our journey to prove that cinnamon rolls can still be steaming hot! These sweet, sexy heroes (and heroines!) are here to save the day, whether it's rescuing their partner from the ghosts of their past or just showing them that they deserve to be loved, cherished, respected...and, of course, pleasured

Princess for a Day

Princess for a Day is a steamy contemporary, royal romance retelling of the Princess and the Pauper, featuring a virgin plus-sized heroine, an LGBTQ+ snarky fairy godmother or bestie, and a prince betrothed to another woman.

True love, royal intrigue, and the adventure of a lifetime await!

Lake Heart

Sometimes your true dream is the one you leave behind.

Milton Keynes UK
Ingram Content Group UK Ltd.
UKHW010924210224
438226UK00004B/110